Copyright © 2004 by Nord-Süd Verlag AG, Gossau Zürich, Switzerland
First published in Switzerland under the title *Als die Schneemänner Weihnachten feierten*.
English translation copyright © 2004 by North-South Books Inc., New York

First published in the United States, Great Britain, Canada, Australia, and New Zealand in 2004
by North-South Books, an imprint of Nord-Süd Verlag AG, Gossau Zürich, Switzerland.
Distributed in the United States by North-South Books Inc., New York.
Library of Congress Cataloging-in-Publication Data is available.
A CIP catalogue record for this book is available from The British Library.
ISBN 0-7358-1965-3 (trade edition)
1 3 5 7 9 HC 10 8 6 4 2
ISBN 0-7358-1966-1 (library edition)
1 3 5 7 9 LE 10 8 6 4 2
Printed in Belgium

For more information about our books, and the authors and artists
who create them, visit our web site: www.northsouth.com

Christmas for the Snowmen

By Wolfram Hänel

Illustrated by Uli Waas

Translated by Marianne Martens

North-South Books

New York / London

It was Christmas Eve and bitterly cold. One lonely streetlamp cast a pale light in the dusk. Beneath it three snowmen stood shivering.

"It certainly is cold tonight," said Jimmy, adjusting the pot on his head.

"Yes, sir, it certainly is cold," echoed Jack.

Junior giggled. "You have an icicle on your nose, Jack," he said. "You look so silly!"

"It's not funny," said Jack.

"Maybe if we move around a little we'll warm up," Jimmy suggested.

"Good idea," Jack agreed.

"Oh, all right!" said Junior.

Jimmy headed off, the pot on his head jiggling with each step he took. Jack and Junior followed him. Down the street they went, across the marketplace, and up to the bridge.

Trees looked like black shadows along the banks of the river. The moon cast a silvery glow on the ice.

"Beautiful," said Jack.

"Yes, sir, beautiful," said Jimmy.

"But I'm still freezing," grumbled Junior.

The snowmen stood and admired the frozen river.

A crow cawed overhead, and muffled church bells rang in the distance.

"Why are the church bells ringing?" asked Junior.

"Because it's Christmas Eve," said Jack. "Did you forget?"

"Of course I didn't," said Junior, who'd forgotten.

"Listen up," said Jimmy. "Why don't we go to church too? We could join in the singing."

Jimmy led the way. A warm beam of light shone through the church windows. Jimmy smiled happily as he pulled open the big door. Eagerly, the snowmen tried to push their way in, but the church was packed with people and there was no room for them.

"We're too late," Jimmy said sadly.

"Yes, we're too late," Jack agreed.

"Now what?" asked Junior.

Across the street was a restaurant.

"Look!" cried Junior, pointing to the sign outside the door.

"Tonight! Christmas Eve Special," Jimmy read aloud.

"Come on, let's go in," said Jack. "I'm starving!"

Jimmy, Jack, and Junior marched into the restaurant and sat down at a table in the corner. There was Christmas music playing. The host was telling stories. And the guests were all laughing and having fun.

"Very nice," said Jimmy, taking off his pot.

"Yes, sir, very nice indeed," said Jack.

TONIGHT!
Christmas Eve
Special

"Uh-oh!" said Junior quietly. "What's the worst thing that can happen to a snowman?"

"Why melting, of course," Jack replied. "You know that."

"That's what I was afraid of," said Junior, pointing under the table.

"Oh no!" Jack cried.

"Let's get out of here!" said Jimmy, grabbing his pot and running out of the restaurant. Jack and Junior followed close behind.

Soft lights glowed in all the windows. Jimmy, Jack, and Junior were once again alone in the empty streets. A freezing wind whipped around the corners, and above them, stars twinkled in the cold winter sky. The only sound was the crunch the snowmen made as they walked.

Suddenly Jimmy stopped short. "This is terrible," he declared. "It's Christmas Eve, and we're miserable. It's so cold and lonely out here, but inside, where everyone else is celebrating, it's too warm for us."

"What if we freeze to death?" wailed Junior.

"Don't be silly. Snowmen can't freeze to death," Jack replied.

The snowmen stared at each other sadly. Suddenly a door flew open, and a light shone across their path. Two children, who had seen the snowmen from their window, came rushing outside.

"There they are!" shouted the boy. "Will you look at that! The big one is wearing a pot for a hat!"

"And that one has an icicle hanging off his nose!" said the girl. "Come, let's fill up the street with snowmen!"

Before long, other doors flew open, and more and more children came running out into the street. Tirelessly, they rolled snowball after snowball, ran to get carrots and straw hats, coal for the eyes, and giant pots and buckets. Their hands were blue with cold, and they puffed on them as they headed back home.

Now there were twenty snowmen on the street, smiling at each other. They gathered closer and rubbed their stomachs together to warm up.

"*This* is more like it!" declared Jimmy.

"There are so many of us!" Junior said in amazement.

"More than enough for a real Christmas celebration," said Jack.

"Merry Christmas to all!" Jimmy called. Then he waved his broom and led all the snowmen as they sang Christmas carols together.

Suddenly, very quietly, it started to snow. First just a couple of flakes drifted down. But soon the air was filled with swirling snow. And the snowmen laughed, danced, and made merry long into the night.

It was still snowing the next morning. Children rushed into the street calling, "Merry Christmas!" They built more snowmen. Then, with Jimmy, Junior, and Jack standing happily in the middle, they all joined in the snowmen's Christmas celebration.

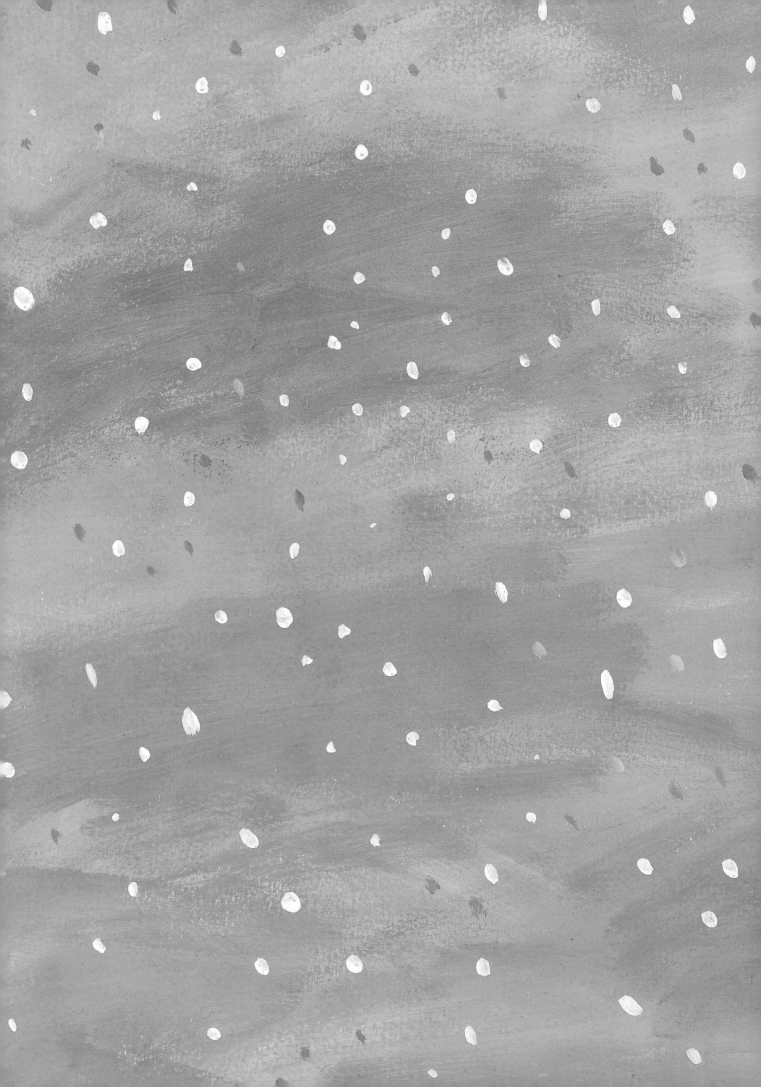